# Away Go The Boats

Modern Curriculum Press
BEGINNING
TO
READ
Series

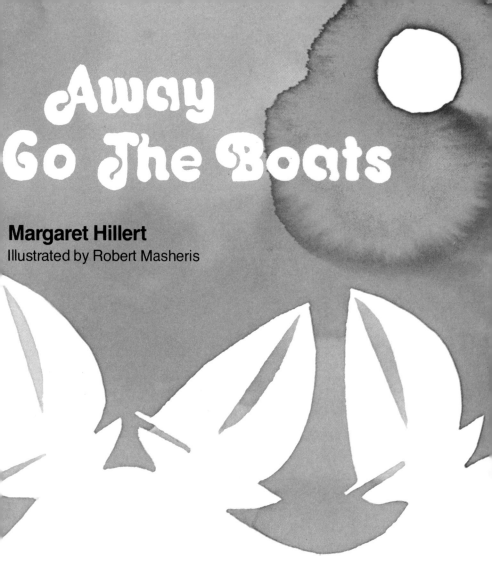

# Away Go The Boats

**Margaret Hillert**

Illustrated by Robert Masheris

**MODERN CURRICULUM PRESS**
CLEVELAND · TORONTO

**Library of Congress Cataloging in Publication Data**

Hillert, Margaret.
  Away go the boats.

  (MCP just beginning-to-read books)
  SUMMARY: During her bath a young girl takes an imaginary ocean voyage to a tropical island.
  [1. Baths — Fiction]  I. Masheris, Robert.
II.  Title.
PZ7.H558Aw      [E]       80-14519

ISBN 0-8136-5573-0 Paperback
ISBN 0-8136-5073-9 Hardbound

  10  9  8  7  6  5  4  3            94  93

Library of Congress Catalog Card Number: 80-14519

Mother said, "Come on now.
I want you to get in here.
Get in. Get in."

The girl said, "Do I have to?
I do not want to.
I want to play."

6

Mother said, "Yes, yes.
Here is something for
you to play with.
Here is a boat.
A little blue boat."

7

"Oh, good," said the girl.
"My little blue boat.
I like this boat.
It is fun to play with."

Mother said, "Jump in.
Jump in, and I will go.
I have work to do.
You have work to do, too.
Do it. Do it."

"This is a good, good boat.
Go, boat, go.
Go, go, go."

10

Now I will play that this boat
is a big one.
I will get on it.
I will go away, away.

Here I am on my big boat.
I can make it go
where I want it to go.

Where will I go?
What will I find?
What will I see?

13

14

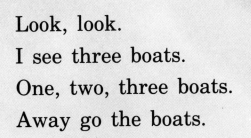

Look, look.
I see three boats.
One, two, three boats.
Away go the boats.

And away I go, too.
On and on I go.
What fun!
What fun!

16

Look up.
Up, up, up.
Way, way up.
Look what I see.

17

Now look at that.
How big it is.
Big, big, big.
How it can jump!

19

Here is a good spot.
I can get out here.
I can look for something.

Oh, who are you?
My, you are a pretty one.
Red and yellow.
Blue and green.

22

And look here.
Oh, what do I see here?
One, two, three little ones.
Three funny little ones.

23

Oh, oh!
You are not funny.
You are too big for me.
I guess I will go away now.

Here I go.
Away, away.
What a good ride this is!

"Oh, Mother.
Do I have to get out now?
I like it here.
It is fun."

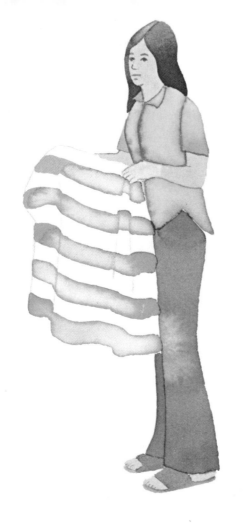

"Yes, yes.
Get out. Get out.
Come out now.
I will help you."

"I will get out, but I will take the boat with me. It is a good little boat."

**Margaret Hillert,** author of many MCP Beginning-To-Read Books, has been a first-grade teacher in Royal Oak, Michigan, since 1948.

*Away Go the Boats* uses the 73 words listed below.

| | | | |
|---|---|---|---|
| a | get | make | take |
| am | girl | me | that |
| and | go | Mother | the |
| are | good | my | this |
| at | green | | three |
| away | guess | not | to |
| | | now | too |
| big | have | | two |
| blue | help | oh | |
| boat(s) | here | on | up |
| but | how | one(s) | |
| | | out | want |
| can | I | | way |
| come | in | play | what |
| | is | pretty | where |
| do | it | | who |
| | | red | will |
| find | jump | ride | with |
| for | | | work |
| fun | like | said | |
| funny | little | see | yellow |
| | look | something | yes |
| | | spot | you |